BOLTS

ADVENTURES OF THE SUPER ZEROES

by Russ Bolts

illustrated by Jay Cooper

LITTLE SIMON

New York London Toronto Sydney New Delhi

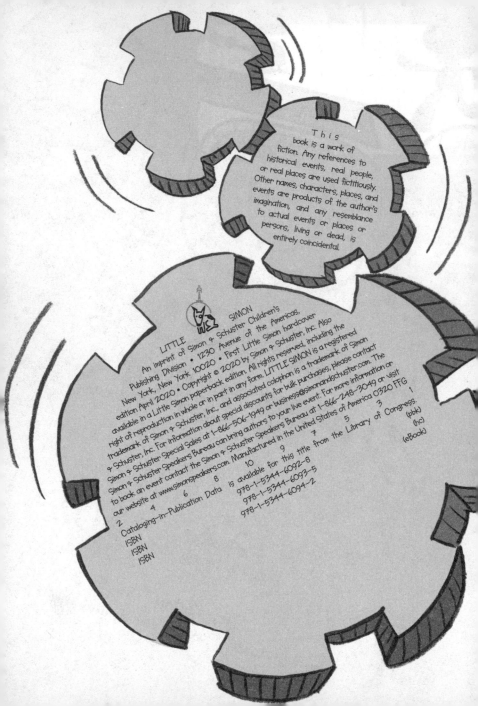

LITTLE SIMON
An imprint of Simon & Schuster Children's Publishing Division • 1230 Avenue of the Americas, New York, New York 10020 • First Little Simon hardcover edition April 2020 • Copyright © 2020 by Simon & Schuster, Inc. Also available in a Little Simon paperback edition. All rights reserved, including the right of reproduction in whole or in part in any form. LITTLE SIMON is a registered trademark of Simon & Schuster, Inc., and associated colophon is a trademark of Simon & Schuster, Inc. For information about special discounts for bulk purchases, please contact Simon & Schuster Special Sales at 1-866-506-1949 or business@simonandschuster.com. The Simon & Schuster Speakers Bureau can bring authors to your live event. For more information or to book an event contact the Simon & Schuster Speakers Bureau at 1-866-248-3049 or visit our website at www.simonspeakers.com. Manufactured in the United States of America 0320 FFG
2   4   6   8   10   9   7   5   3   1
Cataloging-in-Publication Data is available for this title from the Library of Congress.
ISBN 978-1-5344-6092-8 (pbk)
ISBN 978-1-5344-6093-5 (hc)
ISBN 978-1-5344-6094-2 (eBook)

CONTENTS

CHAPTER 1

A Normal Day

Hello, humans! It's another normal day in Botsburg. The bird-bots are chirping.

Grown-up Bots are working.

STOP BOT!

And the student Bots are learning at school.

BOT SCHOOL

Wait! It looks like some students have escaped!

Phew. They are not escaping. They are getting on the school bus.

3

6

9

17

18

21

ON
BUTTON

The music was so loud, other planets could probably hear it.

26

29

31

Costumes

41

costumes!

47

CHAPTER 6

Meanwhile

61

The students continued their tour.

An ice-cream spaceship got stuck before it reache[d] the playground.

The Dragon Bots were watching a play.

The Oozy Goozers moved to the perfect planet.

Shhh, someone is hard at work.

But these are the Bots we should worry about. Watch.

74

84

93

106

109

KA-POW!

Oh, our superhero Bots are in trouble now! I am almost too scared to watch what happens.

Almost.

110

114

Super Friends

Back on the bus, Joe and Rob realized that they didn't need to be super to have great adventures.

They just needed to have super friends.

121